THE AMERICAN GIRLS

17 *64*

KAYA, an adventurous Nez Perce girl whose deep love
for horses and respect for nature nourish her spirit

17 *74*

FELICITY, a spunky, spritely colonial girl,
full of energy and independence

18 *24*

JOSEFINA, an Hispanic girl whose heart and
hopes are as big as the New Mexico sky

18 *54*

KIRSTEN, a pioneer girl of strength and
spirit who settles on the frontier

18 *64*

ADDY, a courageous girl determined to be
free in the midst of the Civil War

19 *04*

SAMANTHA, a bright Victorian beauty, an
orphan raised by her wealthy grandmother

19 *34*

KIT, a clever, resourceful girl facing the
Great Depression with spirit and determination

19 *44*

MOLLY, who schemes and dreams on the
home front during World War Two

1764
CHANGES FOR KAYA
A Story of Courage

BY JANET SHAW

ILLUSTRATIONS BILL FARNSWORTH

VIGNETTES SUSAN MCALILEY

American Girl®

Published by Pleasant Company Publications
For information, address: Book Editor, Pleasant Company Publications,
8400 Fairway Place, P.O. Box 620998, Middleton, WI 53562.

Visit our Web site at **americangirl.com**

Printed in China.
02 03 04 05 06 07 08 LEO 12 11 10 9 8 7 6 5 4 3 2 1

The American Girls Collection®, Kaya™, and American Girl®
are trademarks of Pleasant Company.

PICTURE CREDITS

pp. 60–61—photo by Kathy Borkowski (Wallowa Valley); Sakakawea Statue, C1106,
State Historical Society of North Dakota, Capitol Grounds, Bismarck, ND (Sacagawea
statue); National Numismatic Collection, National Museum of American History,
Smithsonian Institution (peace medal); Idaho State Historical Society, Boise
(MS2/1053/3, 6) (drawing of Nez Perce spiritual images); pp. 62–63— Courtesy Sid
Richardson Collection of Western Art, Fort Worth, TX (*Trouble on the Horizon*, Charles
M. Russell, 1893); photo courtesy of National Park Service, Nez Perce National
Historical Park (Nez Perce chiefs); pp. 64–65— photo courtesy of National Park Service,
Nez Perce National Historical Park (Swan Necklace); *The Long Trail* © Proferes 1999
www.proferes.com (painting); pp. 66–67—Idaho State Historical Society (MS2/1053/3, 6)
(drawing of warriors); MSCUA, University of Washington Libraries (NA 878) (Ollokot);
Idaho State Historical Society (MS2/1053/3, 6) (drawing of Nez Perce women);
Smithsonian Institution (NMNH 2987B1) (Black Eagle); Bettmann/CORBIS (Chief
Joseph); pp. 68–69—Lewiston Tribune, Lewiston, ID (park ranger with tepee); photo by
Antonio Smith (girl dancer); © Chuck Williams, Mosier, OR (girl on horseback).

Library of Congress Cataloging-in-Publication Data

Shaw, Janet Beeler, 1937–
Changes for Kaya : a story of courage / by Janet Shaw ;
illustrations, Bill Farnsworth ; vignettes, Susan McAliley.

p. cm. — (The American girls collection)

Summary: While looking for Steps High, the horse that had been stolen
from her, Kaya faces danger from a sudden mountain fire. Includes
historical notes on the Nez Perce Indians.
ISBN 1-58485-434-0 – ISBN 1-58485-433-2 (pbk.)

[1. Horses—Fiction. 2. Fires—Fiction. 3. Nez Perce Indians—
Fiction. 4. Indians of North America—Northwest, Pacific—
Fiction. 5. Northwest, Pacific—Fiction.] I. Farnsworth, Bill, ill. II.
McAliley, Susan, ill. III. Title. IV. Series.
PZ7.S53423 Cf 2002 [Fic]—dc21 2002018439

TO MY STEPDAUGHTER, BECKY,
AND HER CHILDREN,
TONY AND ADRIENNE,
WITH LOVE

Kaya and her family are *Nimíipuu*, known today as Nez Perce Indians. They speak the Nez Perce language, so you'll see some Nez Perce words in this book. Kaya is short for the Nez Perce name *Kaya'aton'my'*, which means "she who arranges rocks." You'll find the meanings and pronunciations of these and other Nez Perce words in the glossary on page 70.

Table of Contents

KAYA'S FAMILY

TOE-TA
*Kaya's father, an
expert horseman and
wise village leader.*

EETSA
*Kaya's mother, who is a
good provider for her
family and her village.*

KAYA
*An adventurous girl
with a generous spirit.*

BROWN DEER
*Kaya's sister, who is old
enough to court.*

**WING FEATHER
AND SPARROW**
*Kaya's mischievous
twin brothers.*

KAUTSA
*Kaya's grandmother on
her mother's side.*

SPEAKING RAIN
*A blind girl who lives
with Kaya's family and
is a sister to her.*

STEPS HIGH
Kaya's beloved horse.

RAVEN
*A boy who loves to
race horses.*

FOX TAIL
*A bothersome boy
who can be rude.*

SMOKE ON
THE WIND

Kaya sat with Speaking Rain and some
younger children on the dry, yellowed
grass by the stream that wove its way
across Weippe Prairie. For the first time in a long
time, Kaya and her sister played with their dolls.
At the end of summer, *Nimíipuu* women and girls
worked hard to collect as much food as possible
before cold weather came. Kaya couldn't work with
the others because she was still mourning for her
namesake, Swan Circling, and her sad feelings
would spoil the roots and berries. Instead, she
helped in other ways. Today she'd been busy
carrying water, gathering wood for the fires, and
sweeping around the tepees. Then, as the sun had

1

grown hotter and hotter, she and Speaking Rain were given the job of looking after their little brothers and some other small children in the shade of the pines. "Let's pretend we're setting up a camp," Kaya suggested, and the children nodded happily.

First Kaya made split-willow horses so that the little boys could play roundup. Then she made a fire ring of pebbles so that the little girls could pretend to cook with their miniature woven baskets. After that she set up a small tepee frame of willow branches and covered it with several old tule mats. The play tepee was big enough to hold several little girls, and they crawled inside with their dolls.

Kaya and Speaking Rain lay at the tepee entrance. As Kaya smoothed the delicate fringe on her doll's dress, she caught a glimpse of Brown Deer digging camas with the other women. It had been many snows since her hardworking older sister had played games like this one. Kaya knew that someday she would be too grown-up to play with her doll. And although she wanted to be strong,

2

responsible, and a leader of her people, right now she was grateful to enjoy this game with the children.

After the salmon runs were over on the Big River, Kaya's band traveled here to the foothills of the mountains to dig roots, pick berries, and hunt. Speaking Rain would spend part of the year with her Salish mother, who had saved Speaking Rain's life when she was separated from the enemies who held her captive. But until spring the sisters would be together. Now Kaya's strongest fear was that she'd never see her beloved horse again. Although

Toe-ta told her to choose another good mount of her own, she was certain she could never love another horse as much as she did Steps High.

As Kaya thought of her horse, she put a toy horse made of a forked stick into Speaking Rain's hands. "Will you hold this so I can hitch up the travois?" Kaya asked. "Your doll can ride the horse when we've got the travois loaded."

Speaking Rain held the stick horse steady between the poles of the little travois, but instead of smiling as the other children did, she frowned. "The smell of smoke on the wind is growing stronger," she said.

"You've got a nose as keen as a bear's," Kaya teased. She thought that because her sister was blind, her sense of smell was especially sharp.

Speaking Rain lifted her chin and sniffed again. "It smells like a grass fire," she said. "Is a new one burning?"

Kaya shaded her eyes and gazed across the prairie. To the west, the sun blazed above red clouds massed at the horizon. To the east, a thick haze hung low over the Bitterroot Mountains, which she had

4

crossed with Two Hawks after they escaped from
their enemies. When she drew a deep breath,
smoke stung her nose, too. She licked her lips and
tasted ash on her tongue. In this hot, dry season,
lightning set many fires in the fields and forests,
but she didn't see any new plumes of smoke in the
surrounding hills. "Fires always flare up toward
sundown when the wind rises," she said. "Are you
troubled, Little Sister?"

"Aa-heh, I am troubled," Speaking Rain
admitted. "Fire is like a mountain lion—you don't
know when it might attack."

"I'd be troubled, too, if our scouts didn't
always warn us of dangers," Kaya said.

"But our scouts are on the lookout for many
things besides fires these days," Speaking Rain
reminded her.

Kaya knew her sister was right. The scouts
always kept watch for anything that might
endanger the people, but now they were scouting
out game trails and salt licks, too, as the best
season for elk hunting approached. When Kaya
thought of the elk hunts, she felt
a shiver of pride. Toe-ta was

5

one of the most experienced hunters, and the men had asked him to serve as headman for the hunts. Toe-ta's *wyakin*, a wolf, had given him strong hunting power, and the hunters needed to kill many elk to feed everyone through the long, cold season to come. The elk hunts would also be a chance for Cut Cheek to prove his worth as a provider so that he and Brown Deer would be allowed to marry.

Speaking Rain cocked her head. "I hear horses coming this way," she said.

Kaya heard the hoofbeats, too, and got to her feet. "They're coming slowly," she said. "The horses would be galloping if scouts were bringing a warning."

Soon Kaya could see a line of men riding out of the woods on the far side of the prairie. They were followed by women and children on horseback, pack horses, and other women whose mounts pulled loaded travois. Their dogs trotted alongside the horses, wagging their tails as the camp dogs rushed out to meet them.

"It's the hunting party that went over the

6

Buffalo Trail last year to hunt," Kaya said. "Come on, let's welcome them back!"

The children didn't need urging—they were already hurrying to meet the buffalo hunters and the women who'd gone along with them to run the camp and prepare the meat. Kaya grabbed Speaking Rain's hand and they ran to greet them, too.

After everyone had greeted the hunters, and the dried meat and hides had been distributed, the young men took their horses to the stream. When the horses had drunk their fill, the men splashed them with the cool water, then let them dry themselves by rolling in the grass. Kaya and Speaking Rain eagerly joined their young uncles, who always brought news and stories. Tatlo, growing big and long-legged now, left the milling dog pack and pressed himself against Kaya's legs.

Jumps Back tugged Kaya's braid to tease her. He was a short, easygoing fellow with a big grin. After Brown Deer turned him down in the courtship dance and chose Cut Cheek instead, Jumps Back had said he hoped she was happy with her choice. Kaya liked him for that generous thought. "We've been gone so long, you girls are almost grown-up!" Jumps

Back said. "I bet the boys serenade you with their flutes!"

"Not me!" Speaking Rain said with a giggle.

"Not me!" Kaya echoed her sister.

"Do your cousins still call you that silly nickname, Magpie?" Jumps Back asked, nudging Kaya's arm with his and laughing.

Kaya laughed, too. "Nobody calls me Magpie anymore—except once in a while," she said. These days she rarely heard the nickname she'd gotten when she neglected the twins, and Whipwoman switched all the children for her offense. But to change the subject, she pointed to a young stallion getting to his feet, bits of grass stuck in his black mane and tail. "I haven't seen that bay before. He looks fast."

"Aa-heh, he is fast," Jumps Back said. "I chased him hard on my best horse to get a rope on him. Four sleeps ago we came upon a few horses led by a rogue stallion. He drove off his herd before we could get close, but this young stallion hung back from the others, and I gave chase. He'd been driven off by the older horse, I think."

"I didn't know there was a herd of untamed

horses in this area," Kaya said.

"Some seem tame," Jumps Back said. "We think they're Nimíipuu horses. We're going to try to find them again before the snows come."

Kaya's pulse sped. "Nimíipuu horses!" she exclaimed. "The ones stolen from us last year? Was my horse one of them? Steps High has a star on her forehead, remember?" Hearing the excitement in her voice, Tatlo gazed up at her, his tail thumping against her leg.

Jumps Back rubbed his forehead as he thought hard. "I'm not sure," he said. "There were a few spotted horses in the herd, but I didn't get a good look."

"I guess I'm hoping for too much," Kaya said with disappointment. "I last saw my horse in Salish country. She couldn't be back in these mountains."

"Don't be too sure about that," Jumps Back said kindly. "A stolen horse can stray off if it isn't tied to another horse while it gets accustomed to the herd. Your horse could have strayed off and headed back this way, maybe searching for you. If we can track down those horses again, we'll find out."

But Kaya was almost afraid to hope—it would

hurt so badly to have her hopes dashed. Instead, she asked Many Deer, one of her uncles, "Did you make any good trades in your travels?"

"We met up with some hunters from the north," Many Deer said. He was known as a good hunter but was even better known for his short temper. "They wanted to trade for our best horses, but we refused. Instead, we traded a pack horse for three buffalo calfskin robes and some rawhide rope. That was a good trade!" His broad face flushed as he boasted. "And I got something they say came from the east, maybe from men with pale, hairy faces. Look here!" He opened his pack and took out a red-and-white bead, holding it out for Kaya to examine.

"It's pretty," Kaya said hesitantly—she remembered her grandmother's warnings about dangers from pale-faced men.

Speaking Rain was stroking Tatlo. Kaya took her sister's hand and guided her fingertip to the bead. "It's smooth!" Speaking Rain exclaimed. "Maybe Brown Deer could sew it on a gift she's making for the wedding exchange."

Kaya leaned forward to take a better look at the

pretty bead. "Would you trade it to me for a basket of dried salmon eggs?" she asked Many Deer.

At that moment Tatlo thrust his muzzle into Many Deer's pack, seized a small bundle in his sharp teeth, and shook it. Many Deer aimed a kick at Tatlo and caught the dog in the chest, sending him tumbling. "Stay out!" he hissed.

"My dog!" Kaya cried.

But Tatlo wasn't hurt. He lunged to his feet and placed himself between Kaya and Many Deer, baring his teeth and growling, ready to protect her at any cost.

Many Deer stepped back and put away the bead. "Forget it! Magpies have a lot to learn about making a trade!" he said scornfully.

"Aa-heh, you're right," Kaya said quickly. She held Tatlo firmly by the scruff of his neck and tried to think what Swan Circling would have done in a situation like this one. "I'm sorry my dog got into your pack," Kaya said after a moment. "Don't let that spoil your homecoming."

Jumps Back tapped Many Deer on the shoulder. "Come on," he said to the bad-tempered fellow. "We're tired and hungry. The boys will look after our horses while we eat." As they walked away, Jumps Back glanced at Kaya with a look of approval that said she'd handled the tense moment well.

Kaya took a deep breath to settle herself. More and more lately she'd been thinking about Swan Circling, the young warrior woman who gave Kaya her name. Kaya realized that her thoughts were now lighter when she remembered her hero. Perhaps sad feelings would no longer spoil the food that Kaya gathered. She wanted to talk over her thoughts with her grandmother.

Swan Circling

Toward sundown, Kaya found her grandmother and Brown Deer cutting tule reeds in a marshy place at the edge of the prairie. They bent low to cut off the tall reeds. "Here you are, Granddaughter," *Kautsa* greeted her. "Come bundle up these tules so we can take them to the village to dry."

Kaya carried an armload of tules to a sandy spot and wrapped cord around them. "Kautsa, I've been thinking," she said.

"Have you been thinking how to make your dog behave better?" Kautsa asked with a smile. "I saw

Many Deer kick Tatlo when he got into the pack."

Was there anything her sharp-eyed grandmother didn't see? Kaya said, "I was angry about that kick, but I apologized for Tatlo."

"*Tawts!*" Kautsa said. "You must treat everyone well if you want to be a leader like your namesake someday. It's easy to be kind to a pleasant person, but it takes strength to be kind to an angry one. Now tell me what else you've been thinking." As she spoke she cut more tules, passing them to Kaya.

"I've been thinking a lot about my namesake," Kaya said, careful not to say the name of the dead out loud. "I've mourned her death for many moons, and I think my heart feels lighter now."

"Are you sure?" Kautsa asked.

"I'm sure," Kaya said.

Kautsa stood up, put her hand on Kaya's shoulder, and looked into her eyes. "If the time of mourning has passed in your heart, will you join us to pick berries?"

"Aa-heh," Kaya said firmly. "My namesake was always a strong worker. I want to live up to her name."

"Tawts! Let's take these tules back to the

village," Kautsa said. "We need to fix our evening meal."

Brown Deer straightened and slipped her knife into the workbag on her belt.

"We need your help with the berries, Sister," she said as they picked up the bundles of tules. "Brings Word told us this will be the last time she leads us in the berry picking. She's getting too old and her eyesight is failing. She feels it's time to find someone to take her place. Who do you think would be a good leader?"

Kaya knew that for quite some time the women had been talking about who would replace Brings Word. She'd been thinking about it herself. "I think our mother would be a good leader," she said without hesitation. "*Eetsa* is very considerate of others, and she's a good judge of where berries are thickest and when they're ready to be picked. She always leaves some on the bushes so there'll be more the next season. But shouldn't the next leader be one of our chief's own daughters?"

"Not necessarily," Kautsa said. Though she carried a heavy load, she walked with vigorous strides. "To Soar Like An Eagle isn't the son of the old chief, but he's the wisest and the bravest among our men. That's why the council selected him to lead us."

"He showed his courage when he was very young, didn't he?" Kaya asked. She loved to hear stories about warriors and their deeds.

"Aa-heh," Kautsa agreed. "As a young man he was hunting buffalo when a prairie fire swept across the plains toward the hunting camp. The horses bolted and ran away. There seemed to be no escape from the rushing flames—the men were sure to be killed! But To Soar Like An Eagle quickly set a fire of his own and burned a patch of the dry grass. Then he and the others lay down on the hot ashes as the prairie fire passed around the burned-off place. He saved many lives that day!"

Kaya frowned in concentration. She tried to imagine standing her ground in front of a wall of flame in order to set a backfire—would she ever be able to think so fast and act with such courage? "To Soar Like An Eagle is very brave," she said.

"Aa-heh, he is brave, but above all else, he's just and he's generous," Kautsa added. She slid the bundle of tules off her shoulders and placed it near the doorway of their tepee. "Wait here a moment,

"Now it's time for you to wear this," Kautsa said.

Granddaughter," she said as she ducked inside.

Brown Deer and Kaya put down their bundles, too. In a moment Kautsa appeared again, the hat she'd woven last winter for Kaya in her hand. Kaya had planned to wear the new hat this past spring when she dug roots for her First Foods Feast, but because she was in mourning, she hadn't been able to dig with the other girls and women. Kautsa had kept the hat with her own things.

"Soon we'll start berry picking, and after that we'll go with the hunters on the elk hunt," Kautsa said. "You'll need much strength in the days ahead if you're to work as your namesake did to feed the people. Now it's time for you to wear this." She placed the hat firmly on Kaya's head.

"*Katsee-yow-yow*," Kaya said softly, touching the single feather that decorated the top. She was eager to join the others again. And when they went with the hunters farther into the mountains, she might find her horse again, too. She narrowed her eyes as the evening wind carried more ash from distant fires. "I'm ready, Kautsa," she said.

THE ROGUE
STALLION'S HERD

The days were growing shorter now.
Kaya heard owls screeching at night
and saw geese flying high—signs that
the coming winter would be a hard one. But berries
were especially thick and plump this year, and with
Brings Word's leadership, the women and girls were
able to pick and store a great many.

As the berry season came to an end, the band
split up. Many journeyed down to Salmon River
Country to set up their winter village in the
sheltered valley there. Kaya traveled with her family
and the hunting party higher into the mountains for
the elk hunts. The men rode ahead, leading the way,
the women and children following with travois and

pack horses. Raven, Fox Tail, and other young boys brought up the rear, driving extra horses to carry back the meat.

As they ascended the trail, Kaya looked out across steep, rocky hillsides split by stony gulches. Whirring ladybugs swarmed around the horses. The mountainsides glowed with deep green heather and red-orange huckleberry bushes. All around, a blue haze of smoke rose from the valleys and tinted the sky gray with ash. Though cold weather was not far off, the days were dry with no sign of rain—it was still the season of fires. The scouts constantly scanned the mountains and skies for signs of danger.

As the women set up the hunting camp, Kaya helped raise the tepees, then took the twins to where Kautsa and Brown Deer were preparing a meal. The boys were hungry, so Brown Deer gave them some pine nuts to nibble on while the deer meat cooked.

"Speaking Rain was glad to go down to Salmon River Country," Brown Deer said to Kaya.

"Aa-heh," Kaya agreed. "The fires in these mountains trouble her."

"I'm not afraid of fire," Sparrow boasted. "It can't hurt me!"

"Speaking Rain knows better—fire *can* hurt you," Brown Deer corrected him. She placed heated stones into the water in the cooking basket, stirring them so that they wouldn't scorch the basket.

"You must always respect the power of fire, Grandson," Kautsa added sternly as she put deer meat into the boiling water. "Fire is a great gift, but it has its dangers, too. You remember the story of the boy who brought fire down from the heavens, don't you?"

"Tell it again!" the twins begged.

Kaya smiled at her little brothers—and at her grandmother. She thought Kautsa liked to tell stories almost as much as children liked to hear them. And although winter was the proper season for story-telling, Kautsa couldn't resist telling one now.

"Long ago, Nimíipuu had no fire," Kautsa began, sitting down on a tule mat and giving her full attention to the story. "They could see fire in the sky, but it belonged to *Hun-ya-wat*, who kept it in great black bags. When the cloud bags bumped together, they crashed and thundered, and fire flashed through the hole that was made."

"That fire was lightning!" Wing Feather knew this story well.

"Aa-heh, it was lightning," Kautsa went on. "How the people longed to get that fire! Without it they couldn't cook their food or keep themselves warm. The medicine men beat their drums, trying to get the fire down from the sky, but no fire came.

"Then a young boy said he knew how to get the fire. Everyone laughed at him, and the medicine men said, 'How can a mere boy do what we aren't able to do?' But the boy waited patiently. When he saw black clouds on the horizon, he bathed himself and scrubbed himself clean with fir branches to prepare for his task. Then he wrapped an arrowhead inside a piece of cedar bark and put it with his bow and arrow. He placed the white shell he wore around his neck on the ground, and asked his wyakin to help him shoot his arrow into the black cloud that held fire.

"The medicine men thought they should kill the boy so he wouldn't anger Hun-ya-wat. But the people said, 'Let him try to capture the fire. If he fails, we can kill him then.' The boy wasn't afraid. He waited until a thundercloud loomed overhead, rumbling and crashing as it came. Then he raised his bow and shot his arrow straight upward. Suddenly, everyone heard a tremendous crash and saw a flash of fire in the sky. The burning arrow, like a falling star, came hurtling down among them. It struck the boy's white shell, resting on the ground, and set it aflame.

"Shouting with joy, the people rushed forward to get the fire. They lighted sticks and dry bark and hurried to their tepees to start fires of their own. Children and old people, too, laughed and sang.

"When the excitement had died down, people asked about the boy. But he was nowhere to be seen. There lay his shell, burned so that it showed the colors of fire. Near it lay his bow. Men tried to shoot with that bow, but not even the strongest man could bend it.

"The boy was never seen again. But," and here Kautsa touched the beautiful shells that fastened her braids, "his abalone shell is still touched with the colors of flame. And the fire he brought down from the clouds burns in the center of every tepee," she said, finishing the story. Then she fixed her steady gaze on the twins, and the sharp lines between her eyes deepened. "Listen to me. You two must try to be as strong and generous as that boy of long ago."

22

Kaya was glad to hear the old story another time, but she thought again of Speaking Rain's worry about fires. She vowed to keep a sharp watch for them as she searched the surrounding countryside for signs of her horse.

On the day before the hunt, Toe-ta hobbled the lead mare with a rope attached to her forelegs so that she couldn't wander away—he wanted the horses close by so that they could be easily rounded up before first light. He invited the hunters into his tepee to talk over plans for the hunt. Then the men gathered in the sweat lodge to make themselves clean. They thanked Hun-ya-wat for all His gifts and prayed that they would be worthy of the animals they needed for food. Kaya could hear their prayer

sweat lodge

songs rising up to the Creator.

That night everyone slept only a short while. Kaya heard Toe-ta and Cut Cheek rising in the dark to join the other men. They took their bows and arrows and put on headdresses of animal hides to disguise their human

23

scent. Kaya, Eetsa, and Brown Deer quickly dressed themselves. They rode away from the camp long before sunrise while the elk were still out feeding or returning to their bedding place from the salt lick.

Everyone dismounted near the valley where scouts had discovered the elk herd. Raven and the boys looked after the horses while the others went forward on foot. Quickly and quietly, the hunters took up positions at the narrow end of the valley, downwind from the elk. At the wide end of the valley, the women and girls fanned out in a broad V to drive the elk ahead of them toward the waiting hunters. They took care not to startle the elk as they moved slowly forward. If the elk started running, they'd plunge right past the hidden men, who wouldn't be able to get clear shots.

Kaya concentrated on the rustle of the elk moving through the plumed beargrass. She could make out the tips of their antlers, the flash of tan rumps, and the flickers of ear tips. Even in the faint light she could see their tracks on the worn game trails. Birds flew up all around her, and from time to time a woman added her whistle to the birdcalls,

24

making her position known to the others.

Then Kaya remembered that she should be on the lookout for fires, too. She scanned the mountain slope at the far end of the valley. There was no sign of smoke on the plateau there, but shapes moved among the pines, and she thought she heard a distant whinny. Holding her breath, she stood still and peered through the dim light. Gradually she made out horses emerging from the trees to graze. Kaya's heart sped. Could that be the small herd that the buffalo hunters had seen? Could Steps High be with them? Kaya stared hard, but the horses were too far off for her to see them clearly.

Kaya walked slowly forward again, but her racing thoughts tumbled ahead, one over the other. What if she slipped away from the others to get a better look at the horses? Couldn't she run up to the ridge for a better view and be back before the slow-moving elk herd reached the hunters? Or couldn't she get a mount and ride close enough to the horses to whistle for Steps High if she was with them? Maybe she could round up the horses by herself— think how proud of her everyone would be!

Then, right in front of her, a pair of magpies flew

25

out of their dome-shaped nest in a thorny bush. Crying boldly, they swooped upward among the other birds. Like an upraised hand, the sight of the magpies halted Kaya's racing thoughts. No, she must not act in such a way that she could be called Magpie ever again! It would be irresponsible to go after the horses by herself. She must follow in Swan Circling's footsteps and do only what was best for her people. She must work with the others so that there would be food for all. Whistling to signal her place in the group, she drove the elk forward to the waiting hunters.

The hunters' arrows were swift and their aim was true. Many elk gave themselves to Nimíipuu that morning. Then the women and girls prepared the meat to be packed back to the camp, where they would cook some of it and dry the rest. Kaya could tell by Brown Deer's shining eyes that Cut Cheek had hunted well. He'd given the elk he'd killed to her parents as a sign of respect.

Kaya couldn't wait any longer to talk to her father about the horse herd she'd seen at sunup.

She found Toe-ta lifting a heavy bundle of meat onto a travois. Quickly, she described the horses she'd seen. "Jumps Back thinks they're our horses, Toe-ta. Steps High might be with them," she added, trying to hold down her excitement.

Toe-ta put his firm hand on her shoulder. "Daughter, there's not much chance that your horse could be with that herd."

"But there is some chance, isn't there?" Kaya insisted. "Steps High could have strayed off and come back this way."

Toe-ta thought for a long moment. "That's possible. We'll go look for the herd," he said. "I'll ask Raven to come along—he's not needed here right now. Let's see what we can find."

Kaya mounted a chestnut horse and rode out of the valley behind Raven and Toe-ta. They followed a game trail that led upward toward the plateau where she'd seen horses grazing. The sun was high overhead, and heat waves shimmered over the stony hillside. She was sure she'd seen the horses near those pines ahead, but now there was no sign of them. Had the lead mare taken the herd where it was cooler?

27

The trail left by the horses curved around the mountain and angled down the northern side. Kaya's gaze swept across slopes dotted with stunted firs and hunchbacked pines, bent down by past winter snows. Deep gulches jagged down the mountain in every direction. The herd could be in any one of them. Would they be able to find the horses before they had to rejoin the hunting party, now a long way away?

The trail descended more and more steeply, and after a time they found themselves in a narrow canyon where a thick grove of tall firs grew. Spears of sunlight shafted down through the canopy of branches, and the shadowed air was a little cooler here. A small stream snaked through the trees. Toe-ta signaled Kaya and Raven to halt their horses and let them drink.

Kaya slipped off the chestnut horse she rode and knelt upstream from the horses, drinking from her cupped hands. The spring water was clean and cold, and she was very grateful for it. When she glanced up again, she realized that the patches of dappled light in the grove of trees were moving. Slowly and silently, as if in a dream, a few horses appeared in

28

the grove—and then a few more. Coming to the watering place, they stepped around fallen logs. When the lead mare spotted intruders, she halted in her tracks, and the other horses came to a stop behind her.

Kaya got slowly to her feet. Toe-ta and Raven stood, too. Then Toe-ta pointed to a horse barely visible behind the others, a horse whose black forehead was marked with a white star.

"Steps High!" Kaya whispered, almost afraid to breathe. In the same moment that she recognized her beloved horse, a long-legged, spotted foal crowded against Steps High's side—her horse had a little one!

Toe-ta climbed onto his stallion Runner again. Raven jumped back onto his own horse, too. "Whistle for your horse, Daughter," Toe-ta said softly. "She'll recognize your whistle. Call her to you."

Kaya's heart thudded, and her lips were dry. She licked them and managed to make the shrill whistle with which she'd called Steps High so many times. Her horse's ears shot up. Kaya whistled again, and Steps High began to move toward her, the foal following closely. "Come on, girl," Kaya urged her horse. She whistled a third time—just as the air was split by a stallion's scream of fury. The rogue stallion had come down from the hill to claim his herd and protect it.

The rogue was a reddish bay with a black mane and tail. Swift as an antelope, he plunged through the trees and across the clearing to guard his mares. His nostrils flared and his eyes shone with defiance as he screamed his challenge at the intruders. Then he lowered his head almost to the ground, his neck outstretched as he dove at the mares, driving them into a bunch.

Toe-ta had his rawhide rope ready. Raven coiled his rope, too, and began to circle around the milling horses. "Whistle again!" Raven cried to Kaya. "Keep calling your horse! She wants to come to you!"

Kaya repeated her whistle. Steps High swung around, trying to elude the rogue, but each time she swerved away from him, he drove her back with the other horses.

Now Toe-ta on Runner circled the herd in the other direction to distract the rogue. The rogue pawed the ground, snorting and trumpeting to drive off the challenger, screaming fiercely that these mares belonged to him alone!

When the rogue's back was to her, Kaya rode around behind the herd. Steps High made another dash for her, breaking away from the other horses. Kaya swung her rope and swiftly threw it over Steps High's head—she had her horse again! In a burst of speed, Kaya on the chestnut horse rode away from the herd. Leading Steps High, the foal running right behind, they galloped off.

Raven on his horse quickly caught up to Kaya. "Let's race!" he called to her with a grin. "Is your horse still fast?"

Toe-ta came galloping after, and they rode up the valley, the rogue's shrill trumpeting echoing behind them.

Stones clattered from under the horses' hooves as they ascended the narrow trail that led over the ridge. Heading back to the hunting party, they made their way through broad canyons and deep gulches. As they rode, Toe-ta studied the sky and the puffy, misshapen white clouds that rose on the updrafts. He seemed worried. In a narrow canyon, he said,

31

"Wait here. I want to get a look at the countryside from the crest of that hill."

Kaya slipped from the chestnut horse and went to Steps High. Her horse shuddered, then pushed her head affectionately against Kaya's shoulder. Kaya ran her palm down the muzzle, soft as doeskin, and stroked the powerful jaw and sleek neck. She gazed into Steps High's dark, glistening eyes and felt her own fill with tears. "You've chosen to be my horse again," she whispered. "Katsee-yow-yow, my beautiful one!"

The foal nuzzled Steps High's flank. "Raven, look at her foal!" Kaya cried. She smiled at the foal's short brush of a tail, long legs, and big eyes. "Isn't he handsome with all the black spots? Won't he be—"

The sound of a running horse interrupted her excited words. Toe-ta reined in Runner, hooves plowing the sand, and motioned for Kaya to mount the chestnut horse again. "There's a fire just over that ridge. The wind is spreading it this way. We have to get out of this gulch." He kept his voice low, but she heard the warning in his tone.

Kaya glanced at the ridgeline. She saw a plume

"You've chosen to be my horse again," Kaya whispered.
"Katsee-yow-yow, my beautiful one!"

of smoke, but it was thin and white—it didn't look threatening. Three or four small spot fires burned near the top of the ridge, but the grass there was thin and sparse and the blazes no larger than cooking fires. What had Toe-ta seen that alarmed him so?

"Stay with me and keep close," Toe-ta said. He urged Runner ahead on the narrow game trail that ran down the gulch. Kaya jumped back on the chestnut, clasped Steps High's rope tightly, and followed her father, with Raven coming right behind. When she looked back again only moments later, more fires burned from sparks blown into the scrub brush. And now she could hear something hissing and growling in the distance—like a mountain lion, the fire was leaping after them!

CHAPTER
THREE
TRAPPED BY FIRE!

The twisted gulch they rode down was narrow and steep-sided. Kaya rode as fast and as close to Toe-ta as she could, keeping Steps High right behind her. The foal ran, too, his head at his mother's flank. Across the gulch, small fires flapped along the ridge where two winds met, pushing the fire back and forth between them. That side, the north one, was thickly wooded with juniper and fir trees. Kaya knew fire would burn fiercely in the dense trees. The south side, where they rode, was covered with bunchgrass and a few pines scattered here and there. Fire would burn more lightly on this side, though in the baking sun, the air itself felt like fire. Her eyes stung and

her throat burned with every breath.

In a gust of wind, the wavering fire across from them dipped down into the pines. Swiftly, it grew and grew. Kaya watched in alarm as burning pinecones began to swirl through the air, starting spot fires farther down the slope. The smoke blackened and boiled upward. Fire began to growl like a bear as it spread both up and down the slope. Could it keep pace with them as they galloped their horses down the gulch toward the open end and safety on the plain beyond? The frantic horses couldn't be held back—every fiber of their beings wanted escape.

Other creatures also sought escape from the windswept fire. Frightened deer, their brown eyes wide, leaped out of the thickets and bounded to the south side of the gulch, racing up toward the ridge. Jackrabbits came, too, and ground squirrels. Clouds of grasshoppers whirred up out of the smoke. Patches of brush under the trees burst into flame, flushing grouse and quail. When Kaya looked back, she saw Raven lying low on his

horse, one hand cupped over his nose and mouth. Kaya thought only, *Stay with Toe-ta! Take care of Steps High and her foal!*

Fearfully, she looked across the gulch again. Heat waves heaved and buckled above the spreading fire. Fiery pine needles rose up like sparks flying. Burning twigs snapped and cracked. Juniper trees began exploding in the intense heat. But the open end of the gulch wasn't far off now—was it? Kaya coughed and her eyes teared in the bitter smoke. It was almost too hot now to breathe, and fear was another fire in her chest. It was all she could do to cling to her horse as it bolted behind Toe-ta's along the narrow mountain-goat trail.

Then, with a roar, the ground fire on the north slope suddenly exploded into the treetops. Kaya saw the topmost branches become a crimson tent of flames. The trees burned from the tops down, like torches. A high wind gusted up from the burning trees, making the boiling fires hotter still. Wind snapped off branches with a sound like bones cracking. It lifted logs into the air. The fire swirl spun down to the bottom of the gulch and burst across onto the south slope below them. With a stab of pure terror, Kaya realized that now it burned ahead of them, too, blankets of black smoke covering their escape route. The panicked horses doubled back, bumping into each other, rearing and snorting in terror.

Kaya fought to stay on her plunging horse. Steps High reared again and again—would she fall backward on the slipping stones? Would the foal be trampled? Terrified, Kaya thought, *Have I found my horse only to lose her to fire?*

Toe-ta scanned the steep-sided gulch, looking for a possible escape route over the ridge above them, but rimrock created a barrier just below the top. Could they find a way through the barrier? Kaya saw there was no choice—they had to try.

"Stay with me!" Toe-ta shouted over the howling roar. "Don't fall back!" His face was black with smoke and fierce with determination. Did he see a way out of this fiery trap? He gestured for Kaya and Raven to follow as he turned Runner toward the steep slope above them and urged him upward. Raven's horse clambered up behind, its powerful haunches knotted with effort. Kaya forced the chestnut to follow and yanked on Steps High's rope to bring her along. The foal sprang over the rocks like a deer. But could the horses climb faster than the fire? Racing for their lives, they struggled upward.

Ashes, like flakes of snow, swirled across Kaya's sight. Burning embers fell onto her head and shoulders, stinging her hands when she brushed them away. On the loose stones, the horses' hooves slipped backward with each lunge until they gained a broad shelf not far below the rimrock barrier. Then the wind suddenly split the smoke, and for a moment Kaya saw the barrier clearly. Was that slash a crevice, a way through? Could they reach it? Again Toe-ta signaled for them to follow. Raven urged his horse after Toe-ta as the curtain of smoke swung closed behind them.

Before Kaya could follow, Steps High began to rear, whipping her head back and forth frantically. Kaya looked back—the foal wasn't there! Was it lost in the smoke, caught by the rushing fire? Frantic to find her foal, Steps High thrashed her head, tearing the rawhide rope from Kaya's grip. "Stop!" Kaya screamed. "Don't go back!" But, searching for her foal, Steps High had already plunged down the slope and vanished into the smoke.

Kaya tried to rein in the chestnut, turn it back after Steps High, but the panicked horse resisted. Without thinking twice, Kaya slipped off the chestnut, which pushed on up the slope where Toe-ta and Raven had disappeared. Kaya whirled around. Smoke surrounded her on all sides. Through the smoke, the sun was blood red. She stood alone. Her eyes felt blistered by the heat, and she cupped her hands over them. *I must be strong!* she thought. *I must not give up!*

When Kaya opened her eyes, Steps High was lunging out of the blackness, her foal again at her side. She'd reclaimed her young one! As Steps High came near, Kaya leaped to catch the rawhide rope still encircling her neck. With her horse pulling her, Kaya stumbled alongside as they started uphill again. Jagged stones tore at her feet. Her ankle twisted and she lost her footing. She fell uphill onto her stomach beneath her horse's legs. Kaya rolled onto her side. Would the hooves crush her? But Steps High curled her forelegs and managed to bring her sharp hooves down beyond Kaya's head. "Katsee-yow-yow!" Kaya cried. But she knew that on foot she couldn't keep up with her horse. Steps High would have to let Kaya ride if they were both to escape the fire.

When Steps High turned uphill again, Kaya saw her one chance to mount—if her horse threw her off, there would be no second try. Using all her remaining strength, Kaya scrambled onto a boulder, clasped Steps High's mane with both hands, and dragged herself onto her horse's back. Steps High shuddered but accepted Kaya's weight—her horse hadn't forgotten! Kaya rejoiced to be one again with Steps High. But which way should they go? She had no idea. The blowing smoke created a vast black cave with no opening. She'd seen a crevice in the barrier, but where was it? There? Or there? Which way might offer escape? If they went the wrong way, the fire would seize them!

Then Kaya heard a shrill whistle, one high, wavering note that cut through the roar. Could it be green wood singing in the flames? The whistle came again, more urgently. *Here! Here!* the whistle sang. It came to her that Toe-ta was whistling to her, signaling the way. She looked toward the sound but could see nothing. Then a gust of wind knifed through the smoke, and again she spotted the crevice, with a deep game trail leading toward it.

Kaya turned Steps High along the game trail toward the opening. With the foal pressing after, they gained the base of the barrier. Now Kaya felt wind pouring through the opening. Steps High felt the wind, too, and nosed forward, though she balked at the narrow passage. "Go!" Kaya urged her horse. Steps High moved one step, then another. Kaya's knees scraped the sides as they slipped through, the foal following. On the far side Kaya saw the ridgeline right above them. She clasped Steps High even more tightly with her knees and pressed her face into the black mane. "A little farther—we're almost there!" she cried. A few more steps and they had reached the crest.

Still panicked, Steps High started to tear down the other side, stones showering out from under her feet. Toe-ta on lathered Runner was riding hard back up the hill, looking for Kaya just as Steps High had searched for her foal. He swerved Runner, grasped the rope around Steps High's neck, and brought her to a standstill before she could injure herself and Kaya. Steps High's chest heaved, and her coat was

"Go!" Kaya urged her horse.

drenched with lather. The foal's legs shook with fatigue. Kaya slumped forward. Her breath rasped in her throat and her lungs ached from the smoke.

Toe-ta threw his arm around her shoulders. "Rest a moment!" he said. "We're safe here."

Kaya gazed around. The fire didn't threaten them here because an earlier one had already burned off the hillside. Ash-gray patches of sage still smoldered. Juniper stumps smoked. In some places fire had swept by so quickly that it had left scrub brush only singed. Farther down the stony hillside, Raven on his horse made his way to the narrow river below, where deer and elk stood chest-high in the water. He glanced back and raised his hand to her—they'd made it to safety!

"You fell behind," Toe-ta said in his deep voice. "I thought I'd lost you."

"Steps High ran away from me to find her foal," Kaya gasped. "When I caught her again, I lost my way. But you whistled to me! I followed your whistle and found the opening. Katsee-yow-yow, Toe-ta." Her voice shook, and she thought she was laughing until she felt tears running down her cheeks.

Toe-ta wiped away her tears with his palm. "I'm so proud of your courage, Daughter," he said. "You saved yourself, and your horse, too. But what was that whistle you heard?"

"Your whistle," Kaya repeated.

Gazing into her eyes, Toe-ta slowly shook his head. "I was headed for the river when I realized you weren't behind me. Right away, I started back after you. But I didn't whistle to you. That must have been the Stick People. They showed you the way."

"The Stick People?" Kaya said.

"Aa-heh," Toe-ta said. "I think they saw you needed help, and they gave it."

Kaya's head was spinning, but she remembered she must leave a gift for the Stick People. "What can I give them?" she asked Toe-ta.

"We'll leave them many gifts," Toe-ta said. "Now let's get to the river. The horses need water, and we do, too." Still clasping Steps High's rope, he began to lead Kaya on her horse down the burned-over hillside, puffs of ashes rising at their feet.

GIFTS

As the hunting party rode out of the mountains to join the rest of the band in Salmon River Country, the skies turned gray with heavy clouds. Soon the first autumn rains began to fall. After the long, dry season of fires, the rain was a blessing. Kaya pulled her deerskin robe over her head, but she lifted her face to the rain. It would soon turn to snow, but now it bathed her cheeks and forehead with a soft, light touch. The rain dripped from the branches she rode under, raising sweet scents of pine and fir. Drops of it beaded in Steps High's mane and on her foal's eyelashes. Kaya stroked her horse's warm, wet neck and smiled to see the foal, which she'd named Sparks Flying, splashing through the shallow stream.

Even in the rain, the woods around Kaya were filled with color. She saw aspen trunks washed to pure white and the larch needles shining yellow. Ferns had dried to a dark orange, rose bushes were red-leafed, and gilded mosses hung from the fir boughs. A snake slithered across the trail with a green gleam. Blackbirds flocked together for their flight south. Red-sided trout leaped from the stream after insects, and on the opposite shore Kaya saw a brown bear gorging itself on fish.

Now deer and elk were coming down to lower country to forage. As she rode across a clearing, Kaya saw a bull elk running through the scrub brush. He lifted his legs high and tilted back his head so that his huge antlers could slip through the branches as he raced like a scout bringing a message. Kaya's heart swelled. She felt how strongly she loved her beautiful homeland and all the creatures that shared it with Nimíipuu.

When the hunting party reached the wintering place, Tatlo burst from the village dog pack and came running to meet Kaya. Bounding alongside

Kaya's heart swelled. She felt how strongly she loved her beautiful homeland and all the creatures that shared it with Nimíipuu.

Steps High, he barked repeatedly as if to say, *You're back, you're back!* And when Kaya dismounted, he licked her cheek over and over again with his warm, rough tongue.

Kaya turned out Steps High and Sparks Flying with the other horses. Then, with Tatlo at her side, she ran to find Speaking Rain. She had so much to tell her sister.

Kaya found Speaking Rain in the snug winter lodge, twining cord from shredded hemp. Kaya went to her knees in front of her and placed her hands on Speaking Rain's arm. "*Tawts may-we*, Little Sister," Kaya breathed. "I'm here again!"

"Tawts may-we!" Speaking Rain gently touched Kaya's fingers. "Is that pine pitch I smell on your hands? Did you get hurt?"

"My hands and arms got burned by falling embers, but I treated the burns with medicine that my namesake taught me to make," Kaya said. "You were right to be troubled about fires!"

Speaking Rain drew in a sharp breath. "What happened?"

Sitting close to her sister's side, Kaya told how she'd found Steps High in the rogue stallion's herd, and about their escape from the fire. "When we got back to the hunting camp, everyone thought we were ghosts—covered in black from the smoke. Before we left that country, Toe-ta and some other men rounded up the other Nimíipuu horses," Kaya finished.

"And now you're back safely!" Speaking Rain had been listening intently, as though she could feel, and hear, and even see everything Kaya described. "Whistles! Your horse came to you because she recognized your whistle. Then the Stick People saved your lives with a whistle."

"Aa-heh," Kaya agreed. "We left the Stick People a big gift of kinnikinnick."

Speaking Rain clasped Kaya's shoulder. "Tell me about Brown Deer and Cut Cheek. Did he hunt well?"

kinnikinnick

"Cut Cheek's a strong hunter!" Kaya said excitedly. "Our parents agree that he and Brown Deer should marry. Eetsa's going to visit Cut Cheek's mother soon to plan the wedding trade. We'll have the marriage feast and gift exchange

before the snow gets deep. But come with me now!
Don't you want to stroke Steps High again? I know
you love her, too. And you have to meet her foal!
They're the most wonderful horses ever!"

When the time came for the wedding ceremony,
the frozen ground was covered with lightly fallen
snow. Brown Deer and the other women put up a
lodge for the celebration, then began cooking for
the wedding feast. Soon the air smelled
deliciously of roasting meats, kouse and
camas cakes, and berry dishes. Kaya's
mouth watered as she helped carry the
gifts her family had made to the new lodge.
"Here's the last of the bundles, Granddaughter,"
Kautsa said. She placed a large bag filled with dried
roots into Kaya's outstretched arms, put another
under her own arm, and picked up a torch. As she
walked ahead, she left shallow footprints in the
dusting of snow.

Kaya's skin prickled with anticipation as she
followed her grandmother inside the empty lodge.
Now it was cold and silent here, but when everyone

gathered today it would be filled with happy talk and laughter. They'd feast until they couldn't eat any more. Then Brown Deer's family would give woven bags filled with dried berries, roots, and camas to the groom's family—food the women had gathered and prepared. Matching them gift for gift, Cut Cheek's family would give parfleches filled with dried meat to the bride's people—foods contributed by the men.

parfleche

Kautsa stacked the woven bags on top of the large pile of gifts already resting on the tule mats. "There, that's everything," she said with satisfaction. "Now we're ready! Let me light one of these fires to warm up the place a little. I want to stay here for a while, don't you? We've been so busy lately that we haven't had time to talk."

As Kautsa knelt to light the fire, Kaya gazed at her grandmother's kind face. Her black hair was streaked with gray and her forehead and cheeks were deeply creased. Firelight glittered in her dark eyes. "Have I ever told you about the time I got lost on the mountainside—truly, completely lost?" she asked Kaya.

Kaya smiled. She loved her grandmother's stories. "When was that, Kautsa?"

"As you might imagine, it was when I was a little girl, about the age of the twins." Kautsa sat back on her heels as the fire began to crackle and held out her hands to the warmth. "I was walking back from picking berries with my mother when she discovered her workbag was missing. She was upset and wanted to go back to look for it. But she didn't want to carry the heavy berry baskets, so she put them down on the trail and told me to sit by them. She made me promise to wait patiently for her and not to move, not even a little bit. She said she wouldn't be long, and she started back up the trail.

"I sat there for what seemed like a long time. I was hot and thirsty and bored. Mosquitoes bit me, and deerflies buzzed around my head. After a while I got up and began poking around in the bushes, looking for something to do. I walked a little way into the underbrush, then a little farther, and a little farther yet. All of a sudden, I realized I didn't know where I was. I tried to get back to the trail, but I couldn't find it. I was lost! Then I forgot everything I'd been told to do if I got lost. Instead of staying right where I was and waiting to be found, I started to run.

"I ran downhill, thorns tearing at my dress, twigs scratching my arms and my face. There were no trails there, no sign that anyone had passed that way. I thought I would never see my family again, so I started to cry, 'Toe-ta! Eetsa! Help me, help me!' I called to them until I couldn't run any farther. Then I curled up under a bush and sobbed until I fell asleep.

"That's where I was, asleep, when my older brother found me. He was hunting higher on the mountain when he heard my cries. He knew that sound travels upward, so he rode down, following my sobs. He took me to our camp. I was overjoyed to see my mother again! She put willow bark on all my cuts and insect bites. She washed my face and fed me. Then she called Whipwoman to teach me my lesson!" Kautsa laughed, and Kaya laughed with her.

Then Kautsa put her hand on Kaya's. "I told you that story for a reason. What lesson do you think my mother wanted me to learn?"

"Not to disobey her," Kaya answered confidently.

"Aa-heh, that's one lesson," Kautsa went on, "but there was another one. She wanted me to learn to be patient—to wait, and to trust the wisdom of others. That's a very difficult thing to do, for it takes great strength to wait patiently." She thought for a moment, then went on. "Granddaughter, you've already faced many tests of bravery. Your next test will be one of patience, and of trusting the wisdom of our elders."

Kaya frowned. "What do you mean, Kautsa?"

"I'm speaking of your vision quest, Grand-daughter—the vigil you must keep at the sacred place on the mountain," Kautsa said. "If your spirit is clear and you're prepared—and if you can hold on and not run away—then your wyakin will come to you there. But before that happens you'll be hungry and thirsty, and exhausted by fasting and praying day and night. Are you afraid?"

Kaya clasped her elbows, asking herself, *Am I afraid?* She had certainly been afraid when enemies captured her. She had been afraid when she escaped and found her way home. She'd been frightened to think she'd lost her sister, and her horse. And she'd been terrified when she was chased by the forest fire. But what she felt now wasn't fear—it was determination. "I'm not afraid, Kautsa," she said in a firm voice. "I'm ready to meet whatever comes."

"Why, that's exactly what your namesake would have said!" Kautsa exclaimed. "You're more like her than you may know. Soon, I believe, you'll use her name. It will be so good for her name to come alive again!"

Kaya's chest felt warm with gratitude when she thought again of Swan Circling's gift. Kaya wanted so much to take the name of her hero, and now her grandmother felt that the time was almost here.

From across the village, criers began calling out, "Visitors are coming! Get ready to greet them!"

"Saddle up your horse and go meet Cut Cheek's people," Kautsa said, getting to her feet. "I'll light these other fires and make the lodge warm for our feast. Go on now, be quick! We've talked enough."

Kaya ran to get the beautiful saddle she'd received at the giveaway after Swan Circling's burial. Then she hurried to the horse herd nearby.

Tatlo bounded along with her, snapping at snow-flakes and tossing up fallen snow with his nose. Steps High was pawing through the ice for grass with the other horses. When she heard Kaya's whistle, she trotted to her side, snorting white plumes of breath.

Kaya thought her horse seemed almost as excited as her frisky dog. Kaya pressed her cheek to Steps High's muzzle and stroked her horse's chest, feeling the strong, loyal heart beating there. In response, Steps High arched her neck and nudged Kaya's shoulder. As Kaya cinched the saddle tightly,

Sparks Flying crowded against his mother, head high and ears forward as though he were eager to welcome visitors, too.

Kaya swung up into the saddle and settled her feet in the stirrups. "Come on, girl," she said to her horse, and then slapped her leg to signal Tatlo to stay at her side. Urging Steps High into a run, Kaya galloped out to meet the visitors on their horses appearing over the horizon.

Looking
Back
1764

A PEEK INTO
THE PAST

Beautiful Wallowa Valley, one of the best-loved places in Kaya's homeland

In the same way Kaya knew to be careful when she smelled smoke on the wind, many Nez Perce people had visions that warned them to be careful of the people with pale faces who were beginning to come to their homeland.

In Kaya's time, most Nez Perces had heard about these newcomers but hadn't seen them. The very first white people who spent time with the Nez Perces were the explorers Meriwether Lewis and William Clark, who first traveled through Nez Perce country in 1805. Chief Twisted Hair befriended these travelers, drew maps that showed how the rivers could take them to the sea, and agreed to care for their horses over the winter.

*A Shoshone woman named Sacagawea
helped guide the Lewis and Clark expedition.*

The Nez Perces were very interested in the explorers' journals and the way white people "talked on paper." They wanted to learn this language, too, both to add to their own store of knowledge and as a way to bond with these new friends from the East. In 1831, a group of Nez Perces went to St. Louis to see their friend William Clark, who had become the United States Commissioner for Indian Affairs. They told him they wanted to learn his language and asked if he would send teachers to the Nez Perces.

Soon after that, Henry and Eliza Spalding arrived in Nez Perce country. The Spaldings were missionaries who would teach the Nez Perce people English, but mostly they had come to teach about Christianity. Nez Perces eagerly gathered to learn, until Henry Spalding began whipping Indians for what he considered unchristian behavior, such as men refusing to cut their hair. He was nearly driven away a number of times.

Traditional Nez Perce beliefs are symbolized in this drawing from the 1880s. Some Nez Perces viewed Christianity as yet another source of spiritual strength.

Prospectors overlooking an Indian settlement

In the 1840s, white settlers and prospectors, or people searching for gold, began trickling through Nez Perce country on the Oregon Trail. Some were infected with smallpox, measles, or other diseases that killed thousands of Nez Perces. The settlers dug up rivers, cut down forests, and let their pigs eat the camas Nez Perces depended on for food. That trickle of white people became a flood in 1850, when gold was discovered in the Northwest.

In 1855 the U.S. government offered its first treaty to the Nez Perce people. Government officials said they would set aside land called a reservation for the Nez Perce people alone, where no whites could settle or mine for gold. The Nez Perces did not want this treaty. They believed that land was for everyone to share, and no one should be excluded from it. Eventually they agreed to sign the treaty because it became clear that if they didn't, there would be war.

Then in 1860, prospectors discovered gold on the Nez Perce reservation. They urged the U.S. government to redraw the boundaries of the reservation so all the gold sites would be outside it. In May 1863 the government

Prospectors charged onto the Nez Perce reservation to find gold, and the government did nothing about it.

offered another treaty to the Nez Perce chiefs, promising them money, schools, houses, and plowed land, but shrinking the reservation to a much smaller size. This is the treaty that tore the Nez Perce people apart.

At first, all the chiefs refused to sell their lands. Chief Hallalhotsoot, called Lawyer, told the white officials that the 1855 treaty was sacred. "I say to you," Lawyer told them, "you trifle with us. The boundary was fixed. . . . We cannot give you the country, we cannot sell it to you."

The government officials then met with the chiefs one by one. Many still stood firm. Lawyer, however, argued that if the new reservation was large enough, he would agree to it. Many other chiefs were outraged, but the officials ignored them. They made a new treaty with Lawyer and other Nez Perce men, many of whom were not chiefs.

The 1863 treaty cut the reservation to one-tenth its original size (red area on map), giving nearly 7 million acres to the U.S. government.

Nez Perce chiefs Timothy, Lawyer, and Jason (seated left to right). This photo was taken soon after the 1863 treaty.

The other chiefs called this the "Thief Treaty" and refused to obey it. They went back to the places they loved best. Old Chief Joseph led his people back to their beloved Wallowa Valley, the beautiful valley of winding waters. His son, Young Joseph, became the next chief for his band. He never forgot his father's dying words: "You must stop your ears whenever you are asked to sign a treaty selling your home. . . . This country holds your father's body. Never sell the bones of your father and mother."

In 1877, the government threatened the "non-treaty" Nez Perces with war unless they moved to the reservation. The non-treaty chiefs did not want to destroy their people any further, so they began the sad journey to the pitifully small reservation.

At this same time, several young Nez Perce men raided white settlements along the Salmon River. These raids set off several others. The anger that had been bubbling inside many Nez Perces finally boiled over. When the Nez Perce chiefs heard of these killings, some, including Chief Joseph and Chief Whitebird of the Salmon River Band, led their people to White Bird Canyon. They hoped to negotiate peace with the soldiers

Swan Necklace was one of the young raiders who started the Nez Perce War.

there. But the soldiers began shooting before anyone could talk of peace. The Nez Perce War had begun. The Nez Perces defended themselves and forced the soldiers out of the canyon. The chiefs then led about 800 Nez Perces toward Canada, where they hoped they could live safely forever.

U.S. Army soldiers chased the Nez Perces for more than a thousand miles, across the Bitterroot Mountains, twice across the Rocky Mountains, through Yellowstone National Park, and over the Missouri River.

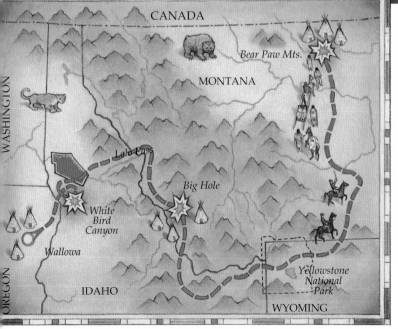

Nez Perces carried all their belongings and drove a herd of hundreds of horses while they fled to Canada.

Warriors parading before the Battle of Big Hole. Their horses have honor marks on their flanks.

In the battle at Big Hole, a valley in Montana, showers of bullets tore through the tepees, pattering like rain. Women and children ran for their lives. Some soldiers killed them accidentally. Others killed them on purpose. The soldiers were told by their colonel to take no prisoners.

After four months of running, Nez Perce elders and children were having a hard time keeping up. The whole group was so grief-stricken, weary, and sick that they had to stop and rest in the Bear Paw Mountains, just 40 miles from the Canadian border.

Women watching the warrior parade. The woman in front may have scars on her arm, a sign of grief after losing a loved one.

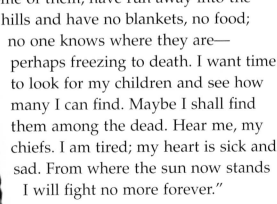

It was there that army troops
attacked them for the last time.
After five days of battle,
four chiefs and many other
Nez Perces were dead. Others
had escaped to Canada, to seek
refuge with Chief Sitting Bull's
people, the Sioux.

The army colonel
promised the remaining
Nez Perces that they could
keep their horses and return
to Idaho if they surrendered.
With that promise, Chief Joseph said these words:
"It is cold and we have no blankets. The little
children are freezing to death. My people,
some of them, have run away into the
hills and have no blankets, no food;
no one knows where they are—
perhaps freezing to death. I want time
to look for my children and see how
many I can find. Maybe I shall find
them among the dead. Hear me, my
chiefs. I am tired; my heart is sick and
sad. From where the sun now stands
I will fight no more forever."

Chief Joseph was never allowed to live
in his homeland again.

When a mountainside is swallowed by fire, the land looks as if it has died. But cooling rains do come, and small green shoots slowly bring new hope and healing to the land. The Nez Perce people, too, are trying to find hope and healing in their hearts. The Nez Perce War scattered them to different reservations and all over the world. Yet, as the Nez Perce saying goes, "Wherever we go, we are always Nez Perce."

Today, the Nez Perce people still reach out to new friends, just as Chief Twisted Hair reached out to Lewis and Clark long ago. Visitors from all over the world come to the Nez Perce National Historical Park in Idaho. Park rangers, both people of the Nez Perce tribe and others from the community, lead visitors on tours, teach them how to build tepees, show them how traditional foods are made, and demonstrate many other things.

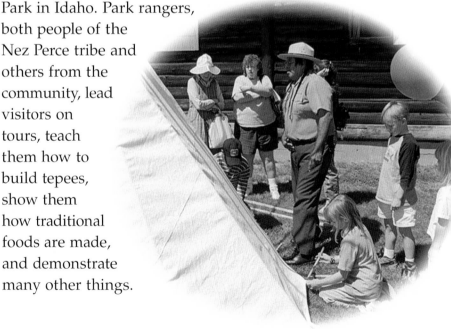

Nez Perce girls still can't resist the beat of the drums!

At Nez Perce pow-wows, all people are welcome and are even asked to join in some of the dances. If Kaya lived among the Nez Perce people today, she'd be happy to see that many of them still live on the same land she called home. She'd be glad to hear her language being spoken, smell salmon roasting on the fire, taste fresh huckleberries, and step inside a longhouse to hear legends and stories. When a magpie alighted on a tree branch, she'd laugh quietly to herself. She'd be especially proud to watch the young girls, so much like herself, parade their beautiful horses in honor of their ancestors, whose inspiring spirits live on to strengthen and nourish all Nez Perce people, each and every day.

GLOSSARY OF NEZ PERCE WORDS

In the story, Nez Perce words are spelled so that English readers can pronounce them. Here, you can also see how the words are actually spelled and said by the Nez Perce people.

Phonetic/Nez Perce	Pronunciation	Meaning
aa-heh/'éehe	*AA-heh*	yes, that's right
Eetsa/Iice	*EET-sah*	Mother
Hun-ya-wat/ Hanyaw'áat	*hun-yah-WAHT*	the Creator
katsee-yow-yow/ qe'ci'yew'yew'	*KAHT-see-yow-yow*	thank you
Kautsa/Qaaca'c	*KOUT-sah*	grandmother from mother's side
Kaya'aton'my'	*ky-YAAH-a-ton-my*	she who arranges rocks
Nimíipuu	*Nee-MEE-poo*	The People; known today as the Nez Perce Indians
tawts/ta'c	*TAWTS*	good
tawts may-we/ ta'c méeywi	*TAWTS MAY-wee*	good morning
Toe-ta/Toot'a	*TOH-tah*	Father
wyakin/ wéeyekin	*WHY-ah-kin*	guardian spirit

MORE TO DISCOVER!

While books are the heart of The American Girls Collection, they are only the beginning. The stories in the Collection come to life when you act them out with the beautiful American Girls dolls and their exquisite clothes and accessories. To request a free catalogue full of things girls love, send in this postcard, call **1-800-845-0005,** or visit our Web site at **americangirl.com**.

Please send me an American Girl® catalogue.

My name is _____

My address is _____

City _____ State _____ Zip _____
12583i

My birth date is ____/____/____ E-mail address _____
             month   day   year   *Fill in to receive updates and web-exclusive offers.*

Parent's signature _____

And send a catalogue to my friend.

My friend's name is _____

Address _____

City _____ State _____ Zip _____
12591i

If the postcard has already been removed from this book and you would like to receive an American Girl® catalogue, please send your name and address to:

American Girl
P.O. Box 620497
Middleton, WI 53562-0497

You may also call our toll-free number, **1-800-845-0005,** or visit our Web site at **americangirl.com**.

‖ ‖ ‖

| Place
| Stamp
| Here

PO BOX 620497
MIDDLETON WI 53562-0497

|․|․|․․․||․․|․|․․||․․․․|․|||․․․․|․․||․|․|․․|․․․||․|․|․․|․․|․․||․|